A MONSTER CALLS

THE PLAY

A MONSTER CALLS
THE PLAY

BASED ON THE NOVEL BY
PATRICK NESS

FROM AN ORIGINAL IDEA BY
SIOBHAN DOWD

DEVISED BY THE COMPANY

WALKER
BOOKS

All performance rights requests should be directed to Michelle Kass Associates

Directed by Sally Cookson, written by Adam Peck and performed by Hammed Animashaun; Nandi Bhebhe; Benji Bower; Will Bower; Selina Cadell; Matt Costain; Georgia Frost; Stuart Goodwin; Felix Hayes; Jonathan Holby; John Leader; Marianne Oldham; Matthew Tennyson; Witney White and Tessa Wood. Based on the book *A Monster Calls*, written by Patrick Ness from an original idea by Siobhan Dowd, illustrated by Jim Kay.

First published 2018 by Walker Books Ltd, 87 Vauxhall Walk, London SE11 5HJ

8 10 9 7

This book has been typeset in Adobe Caslon and Futura

Printed and bound in Great Britain by CPI Group (UK) Ltd, Croydon, CR0 4YY

British Library Cataloguing in Publication Data: a catalogue record for this book is available from the British Library

ISBN 978-1-4063-8713-1

www.walker.co.uk

"Stories are wild creatures...
When you let them loose, who knows
what havoc they might wreak?"

A NOTE FROM PATRICK NESS

I never got to meet Siobhan Dowd. I only know her the way that most of the rest of you will – through her superb books. Four electric young adult novels, two published in her lifetime, two after her too-early death. If you haven't read them, remedy that oversight immediately.

This would have been her fifth book. She had the characters, a premise, and a beginning. What she didn't have, unfortunately, was time.

When I was asked if I would consider turning her work into a book, I hesitated. What I wouldn't do – what I *couldn't* do – was write a novel mimicking her voice. That would have been a disservice to her, to the reader, and most importantly to the story. I don't think good writing can possibly work that way.

But the thing about good ideas is that they grow other ideas. Almost before I could help it, Siobhan's ideas were suggesting new ones to me, and I began to feel that itch that every writer longs for: the itch to start getting words down, the itch to tell a story.

I felt – and feel – as if I've been handed a baton, like a particularly fine writer has given me her story and said, "Go. Run with it. Make trouble." So that's what I tried to do. Along the way, I had only a single guideline: to write a book I think Siobhan would have liked. No other criteria could really matter.

And now it's time to hand the baton on to you. Stories don't end with the writers, however many started the race. So go. Run with it.

Make trouble.

NOTES ON THE PRODUCTION

The following notes are from members of the creative team who worked on the original production of *A Monster Calls*.

DIRECTOR'S NOTE

Just after *A Monster Calls* was published, an actor friend of mine recommended it to me, saying that she thought it would be the sort of thing I'd like to adapt. I bought a copy and read it in one intense sitting and knew immediately that I wanted to adapt it for the stage. I carried it around in my bag for a couple of years whilst making other projects, until a serendipitous meeting with Matthew Warchus resulted in him asking whether I'd heard of a book called *A Monster Calls*, and would I be interested in directing a devised production. I produced the book from my bag and asked, "When can I start?"

We went straight into a workshop to begin the exploration of how to bring this story to life on-stage. I was sure that a big part of how we'd end up telling the story would involve drawing on the imagination of the audience. I'd been struck by something Patrick Ness had said to me in an early conversation – that the tree represents in many ways a father figure who is estranged from Conor in his actual life. It didn't feel right to rely on puppetry to create the tree – I wanted to cast an actor who could provide a paternal quality as well as a monstrous one. Stu Goodwin, an actor I'd worked with several times, felt like a perfect fit – he has a physical power and wildness combined with a deep sensitivity and wisdom.

I suppose the most surprising discovery is that the story doesn't need loads of complex design and props to bring it to life – I'm enjoying testing the theory that less is more. I wanted to find a way to use the ensemble to show what's going on inside thirteen-year-old Conor's head. The inner turmoil he experiences and the gargantuan effort he makes to try to control his emotions is physically emphasized by the ensemble, which has the effect of highlighting his situation and makes it truly theatrical.

Patrick Ness inherited the original idea for the story from award-winning writer Siobhan Dowd, who sadly died of breast cancer before she could write it. He was initially wary of taking on another author's idea, but quickly realized the story Siobhan had started was a trigger to more ideas – he describes the experience as being passed a baton and running with it. The force of that connection between two writers is, I think, a big part of the book's success. Patrick addresses themes of truth, love, grief and how we deal with being mortal in a unique and starkly arresting way. It made me reflect on my own experience of being human and took me to a place of profound sadness, hope and love.

As a company we have dug deep together and I feel very lucky to have been allowed to run with the baton that Patrick has passed on to us.

Sally Cookson

WRITING IN THE ROOM

I thought I would write a note about how this script came into being, about how this show came into being really. Also, I am often asked what I do, what "writer in the room" means, and how a dramaturg works within the context of a devised show. I hope the following words will shed some light on these issues.

My job title is Writer in the Room, but actually a good deal of the writing happens before anyone gets into "the room". Sally (the director) and I work together in advance of rehearsals to create a "working script". This document is a loose adaptation of the book; it divides the book into scenes (which sometimes correspond to the chapters of the book, but more often do not), borrows much of Patrick's (excellent) dialogue and details any ideas we have about what might be happening on-stage at any given point: images, sounds, physical actions etc. It is a very rough first draft – a blueprint, I suppose; its purpose is to give us a firm foundation from which to make the show.

We take the working script into day one of rehearsals and start work – not by reading the script, but by going back and reading chapters from the book with the whole company. We then discuss and interrogate what the scene we are going to be working on might consist of (its content, tone, duration, placement within the play), and then we read the scene that Sally and I have scripted to use as a framework.

The actors then play, improvise and devise, generating new dialogue and new ideas. It is my job to write the script based on what is created. In terms of the generation of dialogue, then, I am one of the writers in the room: everyone within the company contributes.

My role within the "writing" is really a combination of originating, collating and editing material. My main responsibility, though, is to ensure that the show is dramaturgically sound. By that I mean that I try to ensure that what we create in the rehearsal room will make sense to an audience. I look at the arc of the story, the character development, the pacing and rhythm of the scenes, the overall effect of the piece. My discussions are mainly with Sally about what we are making as we make it, and involve constantly scrutinizing and revising the play we are creating together with the company.

The script you are currently holding has been authored by many people. We hope you enjoy it.

Adam Peck

DESIGNER'S NOTE

The original set design for *A Monster Calls* began as a simple, basic playground for the director and the company to discover the language of the production. It immediately asked for a very physical approach to the design and the storytelling, one which would allow a tree to "grow" naturally on-stage and change shape and position with the help of guiding, visible, human hands. In this way the tree becomes as physical and real as Conor himself, neither a metaphysical entity nor part of some "fairy tale", while the proposed open space and limited props invite the audience to add their own imagination to the scenes in the same way that the direct, powerful and economic writing of the original book does.

Michael Vale

COSTUME DESIGNER'S NOTE

Whenever I approach a costume design, I'm always juggling everything that the design needs to answer. Most importantly, it needs to help tell the story but also be exciting, practical, beautiful and work alongside Michael's set design. Designers are like magpies – we are constantly looking for things to draw inspiration from, and for this show I looked at a really wide range of images, from medieval costumes to Christine and the Queens.

I try to work with the company as much as possible to get more insight into their characters and I really enjoy that side of the job. Costume fittings are often a chance for the actors to have a bit of downtime from rehearsals and to process the show from another angle. I also have to work closely with Dan the Movement Director and Matt the Aerial Director to check the costumes aren't going to clash with any physical requirements.

I've designed many shows with Sally, from tiny ones to big-scale productions, but I like to think our approach has always been the same – that is, how can we tell this story in as exciting and thrilling a way as possible?

Probably the most difficult costume to design was the Monster and, although it looks very simple, it is the result of much discussion and gradually reducing it down to what we felt was right for this production and the way we are telling this story.

Katie Sykes

COMPOSER'S NOTE

For me, writing music has to come from deep within. Many people (myself included) have been affected by cancer and family illness, so my starting point was with the original novel, drawing on the feeling I got from it. It's a book that affected me deeply, and still does whenever I read it now. With music, it's so easy to spoon-feed people specific emotions. Sally was clear from the outset that we should avoid sentimentalizing the mother's illness, so it's been an interesting challenge to tap into Conor's heartache whilst respecting her intended vision for the show.

The sound design features a lot of synths, subs and electronic instruments, with a variety of soundscapes, arpeggios, drones and glitchy dark wobbs [synthesizer noises providing a deep bassline]. Musically, I have tried to bleed the themes of Conor's real life into his dreams/nightmares, as I wanted to create a cohesive score throughout the show. There's a progression to the music that accompanies Conor's journey, one which weaves the stories' themes together in quite a filmic way, but is something that hopefully feels entirely seamless. One recurring piece of note is "Conor's Theme" – an instrumental played on the piano, with arpeggios and a drum machine. It's an unusual piece, as the chord progression changes from major to minor chords. In my music I like to create the unexpected, changing the key of a piece for a brief moment or two. I've used this "motif" as a representation of Conor's state of mind, its bending and the relentless stress and pressure he is under.

Benji Bower

This production was produced by The Old Vic in London, in association with Bristol Old Vic.

It opened at Bristol Old Vic in June 2018 before the world premiere at The Old Vic, London, in July 2018.

COMPANY

Anton/Ensemble	Hammed Animashaun
Miss Godfrey/Ensemble	Nandi Bhebhe
Musician	Benji Bower
Musician	Will Bower
Grandma/Ensemble	Selina Cadell
Mr Marl/Ensemble	Matt Costain
Sully/Ensemble	Georgia Frost
Monster/Ensemble	Stuart Goodwin
Dad/Ensemble	Felix Hayes
Swing	Jonathan Holby
Harry/Ensemble	John Leader
Mum/Ensemble	Marianne Oldham
Conor	Matthew Tennyson
Lily/Ensemble	Witney White
Understudy Grandma	Tessa Wood

CREATIVE TEAM

Author Patrick Ness
Director Sally Cookson
Writer in the Room Adam Peck
Set Designer Michael Vale
Costume Designer Katie Sykes
Composer Benji Bower
Lighting Aideen Malone
Sound Mike Beer
Projection Dick Straker
Casting Director Jessica Ronane CDG
Movement Dan Canham
Puppetry Laura Cubitt
Aerial Director Matt Costain
Fight Directors Rachel Bown-Williams and Ruth Cooper-Brown of Rc-Annie Ltd
Voice Coach Charlie Hughes-D'Aeth
Associate Director Miranda Cromwell

Production Manager Dominic Fraser
Company Stage Manager Alex Adamson
Deputy Stage Manager Adam Cox
Assistant Stage Manager Penny Ayles
Costume Supervisor Bianca Ward
Sound No. 1 Tomi Hargreaves

LIST OF CHARACTERS

CONOR

MONSTER

MUM

GRANDMA

DAD

HARRY

SULLY

ANTON

LILY

MISS GODFREY

MR MARL

KING

PRINCE

QUEEN

FARMER'S DAUGHTER

APOTHECARY

PARSON

PARSON'S DAUGHTERS

NURSE

NOTE ON THE ENSEMBLE

The ENSEMBLE are present on-stage throughout. They watch the action and enable the audience to access CONOR's inner world, emphasizing CONOR's emotional state. The ENSEMBLE also become part of the action, creating and populating the environments in which CONOR finds himself, becoming VILLAGERS, PUPILS etc. When individual members of the ENSEMBLE are required to play characters, they prepare their costumes, props etc. in full view of the audience.

ACT ONE

(CONOR enters.)

(The ENSEMBLE enter, cross the performance space and sit down on chairs along the edges of the performance space.)

1.
PAST/PRESENT

(The past, just over thirteen years ago.)

(CONOR's YOUNGER MUM enters, carrying and comforting a baby.)

(CONOR watches her.)

(YOUNGER MUM goes to the window and looks out into the back garden.)

YOUNGER MUM Look. You see that tree, Conor... It's a yew tree. And it's very, very old. Look how big it is... And how small you are! You and I will never grow as old as that tree, Conor. It's ancient.

(YOUNGER MUM moves away from the window and the baby disappears.)

(YOUNGER MUM puts on a dressing gown and transforms into present-day MUM.)

(The past, about eighteen months ago.)

(MUM puts on a headscarf, then exits.)

MUM *(From off)* Night, Conor. Get your head down, love – you've got school in the morning.

CONOR Night, Mum. Sleep well.

2.
THE NIGHTMARE

(Sunday night. CONOR's bedroom.)

(CONOR falls asleep and has a nightmare. The ENSEMBLE create the nightmare – a collage of abstract aural and physical elements from the full nightmare. The full nightmare occurs during Scene 29, The Fourth Tale.)

CONOR   Go away!

(CONOR wakes up.)

                 Go away…

(Pause)

MUM   *(From off)* Conor?! Is that you? Is everything all right?

CONOR   Sorry, Mum, I didn't mean to wake you. I was just … dreaming.

MUM   *(From off)* Are you OK?

CONOR   Fine, Mum – see you in the morning.

MUM   *(From off)* Night then.

(CONOR looks at his alarm clock. It is 12.07 a.m.)

ENSEMBLE   12.07.

(CONOR goes to his bedroom window and opens it. He breathes in some fresh air, but then hears the sound of the wind blowing through the leaves of the yew tree outside. The sound unnerves him. The ENSEMBLE turn to look out of the window.)

MONSTER   *(From off, whispered)* Conor…

(Pause)

                 Conor…

(Pause)

I'm coming to get you, Conor O'Malley.

(CONOR slams the window shut.)

3.
BREAKFAST

(Monday morning. CONOR's bedroom.)

(The sound of an alarm clock.)

(CONOR prepares for school, putting on trousers, shirt, tie, socks, shoes and blazer, packing his rucksack with pencil-case and workbooks.)

(CONOR goes into the kitchen, switches on the kettle and the radio, and looks out of the window.)

(CONOR takes a carton of juice from the fridge and drinks it. He takes a bowl from one cupboard, a box of Shreddies from another, and milk from the fridge, and prepares his breakfast.)

(CONOR sits on a chair, picks up a spoon and eats his breakfast.)

(CONOR finishes his breakfast, puts the bowl and spoon away, and gets ready to leave for school.)

(MUM enters and goes to the kettle.)

MUM   Morning, Con.

CONOR   Hi, Mum.

MUM   Do you want a cup of tea?

CONOR   No, I've got to go – but I boiled the kettle.

MUM   Thanks, love.

(MUM pours herself a cup of tea.)

             You've had breakfast?

CONOR   Yes, Mum.

MUM   You're sure?

CONOR   Yes, Mum – Shreddies and juice. I put the dishes in the dishwasher.

MUM   And put the washing on. Sorry I wasn't up.

CONOR   It's OK.

MUM   It's just this new round of—

CONOR   It's OK.

(CONOR picks up his rucksack and goes to exit.)

MUM   Were you all right last night?

CONOR   Err, fine. Probably just … talking in my sleep or something.

(Beat)

MUM   I forgot to tell you, your grandma's coming by tomorrow.

CONOR   *(Throwing rucksack to floor)* Aw, Mum!

MUM   I know. But you're thirteen – you can't be expected to do the housework every morning.

CONOR   Every morning?! How long is she going to be here?

MUM   Conor...

CONOR   We don't need her here.

MUM   You know how I get at this point in my—

CONOR   We've been OK so far.

MUM   I know you don't like giving up your room and I'm sorry—

CONOR   It's not just giving up my room – she treats me like I'm her employee or something.

MUM   I wouldn't have asked her if I didn't need her to come. All right? *(Beat)* It's only for a couple of days.

(CONOR picks up his rucksack.)

> She's going to bring me some of her old wigs. Can you imagine? I could go blonde, Con. Or curly, or redhead. What do you think?

CONOR   I'm going to be late, Mum.

MUM   All right, sweetheart. See you later.

(CONOR goes to exit, then turns to look at MUM.)

> *(Elsewhere)* There's that old yew tree.

(MUM exits.)

4.
SCHOOL

(Monday lunchtime. School playground.)

(HARRY, SULLY and ANTON enter.)

HARRY   Conor O'Malley! Where did you creep in from? *(Beat)* You see there's something that's been bugging me for a long while now and I've really just gotta get it off my chest. You see the thing I've been wondering is … where did you get them shoes?

SULLY   *(Laughing)* "Where did you get them shoes?"!

(HARRY and SULLY laugh. ANTON stands quietly.)

HARRY   'Cos I'm hoping you didn't pick them yourself. I mean, them shoes are so ugly Sully's dad wouldn't even wear them. And he wears Crocs!

(SULLY laughs. HARRY turns on ANTON.)

> Did you not find that funny, Anton?

ANTON   Yeah.

HARRY   So why aren't you laughing then? Because when somebody thinks something's funny they—

(CONOR goes to leave.)

        (To CONOR) Hey! Where do you think you're going, O'Malley? Playtime isn't over yet.

(HARRY approaches CONOR.)

        How are we today then, O'Malley?

CONOR   Fine thanks.

HARRY   "Fine thanks." Fine's good. Fine's really good.

(HARRY pushes CONOR to ANTON.)

        Come on, Anton, send him back.

(ANTON joins in, then SULLY, pushing CONOR about.)

        Send him back, come on. Send him back. Let's play us some O'Malley ping-pong!

(After a few more pushes, HARRY grabs hold of CONOR.)

        How about now, O'Malley? How are you feeling now?

(HARRY pushes CONOR to the ground, violently.)

(LILY enters.)

LILY   Leave him alone!

SULLY   Oh, your poodle's here to save you!

(CONOR stays on the ground, touching his lip, testing for blood.)

LILY   I'm just making it a fair fight.

SULLY   Go on then.

(SULLY grabs LILY's rucksack.)

LILY   *(Holding on to the rucksack)* Get off!

(LILY goes to CONOR.)

        (To CONOR) You all right?

(CONOR stands, still touching his lip.)

        Conor, you're bleeding!

HARRY   *(Mocking)* "Oh Conor, you're bleeding. You're bleeding,
                 Conor." *(To ANTON)* What should he do Anton? *(Beat)*
                 Anton, did you not hear me? What should he do?

SULLY   Anton.

HARRY   Come on, big man, open your mouth and say
                 something!

SULLY   Anton, will you say something!

HARRY   Come on, Anton, what should he do?!

(ANTON doesn't know what to say, then blurts out…)

ANTON   He should get his bald mother to kiss it better
                 for him!

(LILY punches ANTON and he falls to the floor.)

(The deputy headteacher, MISS GODFREY, enters.)

MISS GODFREY   Lillian Andrews!

LILY   They started it, Miss.

MISS GODFREY   I don't want to hear it. We do not tolerate violence in
                 this school.

(ANTON gets to his feet.)

                 (To ANTON) Are you all right, Anton?

HARRY   No, Miss, he looks like he might have some serious
                 swelling to the brain. He's gonna need an ambulance.

MISS GODFREY   *(To HARRY)* Don't milk it. *(To ANTON)* Anton, get
                 yourself to the nurse. *(To LILY)* My office, Lillian.

LILY   But, Miss, they were talking—

MISS GODFREY   Now, Lillian!

LILY   They were making fun of Conor's mum!

MISS GODFREY   Is this true, Conor?

(Pause)

CONOR   No, Miss, it's not true.

MISS GODFREY   Get to your forms. Go!

HARRY   Yes, Miss.

(ANTON and SULLY exit. HARRY goes to CONOR.)

               Well done O'Malley.

(HARRY exits.)

MISS GODFREY   Lillian, my office! Now!

(LILY exits.)

               Conor? How are things at home?

CONOR   Fine, Miss.

(MISS GODFREY exits.)

5.
LIFE WRITING

(Monday afternoon. School classroom.)

(CONOR, HARRY, ANTON and SULLY take their places in the class.)

(The ENSEMBLE become PUPILS.)

(MR MARL enters.)

MR MARL   *(Quietening the pupils)* Thank you, Year Eight. And thank you, Anton, for your excellent suggestion. So, why do we think Anton's idea might be a suitable subject matter for—

(LILY enters and takes her place in the class.)

               Ah, "But soft, what light through yonder window breaks" – Lillian Andrews, good morning, very nice of you to join us.

LILY   I was talking to Miss Godfrey, sir.

SULLY   *(Mocking)* "I was talking to Miss Godfrey, sir."

MR MARL   *(To LILY)* Of course you were. *(To SULLY)* Thank
               you. *(To LILY)* We were just discussing Anton's
               idea for our upcoming life writing assignment. *(To
               ANTON)* Can you share your idea with Lily, please,
               Anton?

ANTON   I was just saying about when we had a funeral for my
               dead hamster, and I made a speech and that.

MR MARL   And that will be a very sad story indeed. *(Beat)*
               Anyone else?

(SULLY puts up her hand.)

               Jessica?

SULLY   Yeah, I was thinking that ... I could write about how
               everyone thinks I'm five foot four, but actually I'm
               five foot five.

(The PUPILS react.)

MR MARL   You could, yes.

(HARRY puts up his hand.)

               Harry, save us, please.

HARRY   I'm gonna write about one time in PE, when Sully
               sneezed so hard that a nugget of do-do dropped out
               of her bottom.

*(The PUPILS – except SULLY – laugh hysterically, then suddenly go silent
and turn towards CONOR and stare at him.)*

(MUM enters, laughing, and crosses the space. CONOR watches her.)

(MUM exits.)

*(The PUPILS return to normal. The school bell rings. The PUPILS move
to another classroom.)*

*(The sounds from a boring biology lesson. The PUPILS copy something
from the whiteboard in silence. The sounds begin to distort and become
sounds from CONOR's past.)*

(MUM enters and goes to CONOR. MUM strokes CONOR's hair.)

(The school bell rings again, marking the end of the school day. MUM exits. The PUPILS exit.)

(CONOR picks up his rucksack and rushes off.)

6.
LILY

(LILY chases after CONOR.)

LILY	Hey! Hey, Conor, wait!

(CONOR stops, reluctantly.)

	Why did you do that today?
CONOR	Leave me alone.
LILY	Why didn't you tell Miss Godfrey what really happened? Why did you let me get into trouble?
CONOR	Why did you butt in when it was none of your business?
LILY	I was trying to help you.
CONOR	I don't need your help. I was doing fine on my own.
LILY	No, you weren't – you were bleeding.
CONOR	It's none of your business.
LILY	I've got detention all week. And a note home to my mum.
CONOR	That's not my problem.
LILY	But it's your fault.
CONOR	It's your fault! It's all your fault!

(Pause)

LILY	We used to be friends.

CONOR   Yeah – used to be! Until you got such a big mouth!

(CONOR rushes away again.)

LILY   Conor!

(LILY chases him.)

        Conor, will you wait!

(CONOR turns to face LILY.)

CONOR   Just leave me alone, Lily!

(LILY exits.)

(The walls begin to shake and the floor tremors.)

(CONOR changes his clothes for bed.)

7.
A MONSTER CALLS

(Monday night. CONOR's bedroom.)

MUM   *(From off)* Night, Con. See you in the morning.

CONOR   Night, Mum. Sleep well.

(The nightmare.)

CONOR   Go away!

(CONOR wakes up.)

        Go away!

(CONOR checks the time on his alarm clock. It is 12.07.)

ENSEMBLE   12.07.

(Pause)

MONSTER   *(From off, whispered)* Conor…

CONOR   What was that?! *(Beat)* I'm awake. I'm in my bedroom. There's the window. I'm awake.

(Pause)

MONSTER   *(From off, louder whisper)* Conor…

CONOR   It's the wind. It's just the wind shushing the curtains.

MONSTER   *(From off, half-voice)* Conor.

CONOR   All right, it's not the wind – it's definitely a voice. *(Beat)* Don't be stupid – monsters are for babies, monsters are for bed-wetters, monsters are for—

(CONOR is aware of something approaching outside.)

MONSTER   *(From off, louder voice)* Conor.

(CONOR goes to the window and looks out.)

(The MONSTER enters and creaks into life, slowly.)

         Conor O'Malley! I have come to get you, Conor O'Malley.

CONOR   So come and get me then.

MONSTER   What did you say?!

CONOR   I said, come and get me then.

(The MONSTER roars.)

         Shout all you want – I've seen worse.

(The MONSTER goes to roar again, but stops.)

MONSTER   You really aren't scared, are you?

CONOR   No. Not of you, anyway.

MONSTER   You will be, before the end.

(The MONSTER roars.)

CONOR   What do you want from me?

MONSTER   It is not what I want from you, Conor O'Malley. It's what you want from me.

CONOR   I don't want anything from you!

MONSTER   Not yet. But you will.

CONOR   What are you?

MONSTER   I am not a "what"! I'm a "who"!

CONOR   Who are you, then?

MONSTER   Who am I? Who am I?! I am the ancient yew tree! And I have as many names as there are years to time itself! *(Beat)* I am Herne the Hunter! I am the eternal Green Man! *(Beat)* I am the spine on which mountains hang! I am the tears that rivers cry! I am the wolf that kills the stag, the spider that kills the fly! I am the snake of the world devouring its own tail! I am everything untamed and untameable! I am this wild earth, come for you, Conor O'Malley.

CONOR   You're just a tree – with branches and berries.

MONSTER   I do not often come walking, boy – only for matters of life and death. I will be listened to!

CONOR   What do you want with me?

MONSTER   Here is what will happen, Conor O'Malley. I will come to you again on further nights. And I will tell you three stories – three tales from when I walked before.

CONOR   Yeah sure, because that's what monsters always do – tell stories.

MONSTER   Stories are the wildest things of all! Stories chase and bite and hunt. And when I have finished my three stories, you will tell me a fourth. And it will be the truth.

CONOR   The truth?

MONSTER   Your truth – the one you hide, Conor O'Malley – the thing you are most afraid of.

(Sounds from the nightmare.)

You will tell the truth, for that is why you called me.

CONOR   And what if I don't?

MONSTER   Then I will eat you alive.

(The MONSTER approaches CONOR, threateningly, then recedes.)

8.
GRANDMA

(Tuesday morning. CONOR's bedroom.)

(The sound of an alarm clock.)

(CONOR goes to the window and looks out.)

(CONOR changes into his school uniform; in doing so, he finds several yew tree berries in his shoes, which he tips onto the floor. The MONSTER watches him.)

MUM   *(From off)* Con, are you up? Don't want to be late for school.

(CONOR tidies the berries into his rucksack.)

CONOR   Yes, Mum, I'm just getting my bag together.

(Time passes. We hear sounds from CONOR's school day.)

(Tuesday afternoon. CONOR's house. CONOR arrives back from school. GRANDMA and MUM are in the sitting room. GRANDMA has a carrier bag next to her.)

GRANDMA   How was school, young man?

CONOR   Fine.

GRANDMA   You know there's a tremendous independent boys' school not half a mile from me.

MUM   He's happy where he is, Mum. Aren't you, Con?

GRANDMA   The academic standards are quite high, much higher than the comprehensive, I'm sure.

CONOR   I'm fine where I am.

(GRANDMA goes to CONOR and pinches his cheeks, hard.)

GRANDMA   Are you being a good boy for your mum, though?

MUM   He's been very good, Mum – so there's no need to inflict quite so much pain.

GRANDMA   Oh, nonsense.

(GRANDMA slaps CONOR on his cheeks, playfully but hard. CONOR stands and takes it.)

CONOR   Grandma?!

GRANDMA   Go and put the kettle on for your mum and me.

(CONOR goes towards the kitchen.)

               (Grabbing the carrier bag) Oh Bea … wigs.

MUM   Conor, Grandma brought me her wigs.

(CONOR turns.)

               Do you want to see?

GRANDMA   Yes, look.

(GRANDMA takes a wig from the carrier bag and inspects it.)

               Now, when was this…? 1968 or something.

(GRANDMA puts on the wig.)

MUM   When you were burning your bra.

CONOR   Mum!

MUM   What? I just said bra.

GRANDMA   *(Presenting herself, wigged)* Cathy McGowan.

CONOR   Who's Cathy McGowan?

GRANDMA   Cathy McGowan. *(To MUM)* "Ready, Steady, Go"?

MUM   I've no idea.

GRANDMA   Oh, you're so young.

(GRANDMA removes her wig, then takes out another wig and hands it to MUM.)

             What about this?

MUM   Oh, very glam!

(MUM tries on the wig.)

             When did you wear this?

GRANDMA   Never you mind. *(To CONOR)* Marilyn … Monroe.

(MUM starts singing "I Wanna Be Loved by You" by Herbert Stothart, Harry Ruby and Bert Kalmar.)

(CONOR goes towards the kitchen.)

             (Calling after him) Black tea please!

(CONOR goes into the kitchen.)

             With lemon if you have it!

CONOR   As if I don't remember.

GRANDMA   What was that?

CONOR   Nothing.

(MUM stops singing.)

(CONOR prepares cups of tea.)

GRANDMA   *(Referring to the wigs)* So, what do you think, darling?

MUM   *(Removing the wig)* Mum, don't be ridiculous – I can't wear these.

GRANDMA   No.

MUM   No.

GRANDMA   Oh Bea, darling, what are we going to do with you? *(Beat)* Now, we need to have a talk about what's going—

MUM   No, we don't need to have a talk—

GRANDMA   Yes, we absolutely do. We—

MUM   No, we absolutely don't. *(Beat)* Sorry, Mum, I'm
                going to have to go and lie down.

GRANDMA   Right. Of course.

(MUM stands up to leave.)

MUM   Thank you for the wigs.

GRANDMA   You go on then.

(MUM exits.)

                (Calling after her) I'll bring you up a hot-water bottle.

(GRANDMA goes into the kitchen.)

(CONOR hands the cup of tea to GRANDMA, roughly.)

                (Taking the cup) Thank you.

*(GRANDMA prepares a hot-water bottle, then stands watching CONOR
drying crockery with a tea towel.)*

                You and I need to have a talk, my boy.

CONOR   I've got a name, you know. And it's not "my boy".

GRANDMA   That is enough.

(Pause)

                I'm not your enemy, Conor – I'm here to help your
                mum.

CONOR   I know why you're here.

GRANDMA   *(Taking the tea towel from CONOR)* I'm here because
                thirteen-year-old boys shouldn't be doing the
                washing-up without being asked to first.

CONOR   Why, were you going to do it?

GRANDMA   Conor—

CONOR   Just go. We don't need you here.

(CONOR folds laundry from a washing basket.)

GRANDMA   We need to talk about what is going to happen —

CONOR   No, we don't. She's always sick after the treatments. She'll be better tomorrow. And then you can go home.

GRANDMA   She'll seem better tomorrow, Conor, but she won't be.

CONOR   The treatments are making her better – that's why she goes.

GRANDMA   You need to talk to her about this. *(To herself)* She needs to talk to you about this.

CONOR   About what?

GRANDMA   About you coming to live with me.

(Beat)

CONOR   I'm not going to live with you.

GRANDMA   Conor —

CONOR   I'm never going to live with you!

GRANDMA   Yes, you are. I'm sorry, but you are. I know your mother's trying to protect you, but it is vitally important for you to know that when … this is all over, there'll be a home for you, my boy – with someone who'll love you and care for you.

CONOR   When this is all over, you'll leave and we'll be fine.

MUM   *(From off)* Mum…?

GRANDMA   *(Shouting off)* Yes…

MUM   *(From off)* Mum…?

GRANDMA   *(Shouting off)* Yes, it's OK, darling! I'm coming… I'm coming!

(GRANDMA exits, carrying the hot-water bottle.)

(The sound of MUM retching, off.)

(CONOR angrily stuffs the laundry back into the basket. The MONSTER watches him.)

9.
THE WILDNESS OF STORIES

(Tuesday night.)

(The MONSTER is waiting in the darkness. The clock turns to 12.07.)

ENSEMBLE   12.07.

MONSTER   Hello again, Conor. It is time for me to tell you the first tale. Are you listening?

CONOR   No!

MONSTER   I have been alive as long as this land! You will pay me the respect I am owed!

CONOR   What do you know? What do you know about anything?

MONSTER   I know about you, Conor O'Malley.

CONOR   No you don't. If you did, you'd know I don't have time to listen to stupid, boring stories from some stupid, boring tree that isn't even real.

MONSTER   Oh, did you dream the yew tree berries on your bedroom floor?

CONOR   Who cares?! They're just stupid berries! Woo-hoo, so scary! Please, please save me from the berries.

MONSTER   How strange – the words you say tell me you are scared of the berries, but your actions seem to suggest otherwise.

CONOR   You're as old as the land and you've never heard of sarcasm?

MONSTER   People usually know better than to speak it to me.

CONOR   Can't you just leave me alone?

MONSTER   Why are you not afraid of me?

CONOR   You're just a tree.

MONSTER   And you have worse things to be frightened of.

(Pause)

CONOR   I thought... I saw you watching me earlier when
               I was fighting with my grandma and I thought...

MONSTER   What?! What did you think?

CONOR   Forget it.

MONSTER   You thought I might be here to help you. You
               thought I might have come to topple your enemies,
               slay your dragons. When I said that you had called
               for me – that you were the reason I had come
               walking – you felt the truth of it, did you not?

CONOR   But all you want to do is tell me stories.

MONSTER   When you let stories loose, who knows what havoc
               they may wreak? *(Beat)* Let me tell you about the
               end of a wicked queen and how I made sure she was
               never seen again.

(Pause)

CONOR   Go on.

10.
THE FIRST TALE

(The ENSEMBLE transform the space.)

MONSTER   Long ago, before this was a town with roads, cars
               and trains, it was a green place.

(The ENSEMBLE present a forest.)

Trees covered every hill, shaded every stream and protected every house, for there were houses here even then, made of stone and earth. This was a kingdom.

(A KING emerges from the ENSEMBLE.)

A kingdom in which the king and his sons fought dragons and giants, ogres and wizards.

(The KING holds a baby.)

CONOR   This sounds like a rubbish fairy tale.

(The ENSEMBLE lurch towards CONOR.)

MONSTER   Be quiet! And listen. *(Beat)* War ravaged the king's family until he was left with only his infant grandson. *(Beat)* What does a man do when he has more sadness than he can bear alone?

(A PRINCESS emerges from the ENSEMBLE.)

A princess from a far-off kingdom took pity on him.

(The PRINCESS approaches the KING, suspiciously.)

They were married quickly, even though no one really knew who this strange woman was.

(The PRINCESS is crowned and becomes the QUEEN.)

Time passed until the prince was within two years of his eighteenth birthday – the age at which he could inherit the throne.

(The PRINCE emerges from the ENSEMBLE and replaces the baby.)

These were happy days for the kingdom. *(Beat)* But rumour began that the queen had conjured grave magicks. And with still a year left before the prince was old enough to take the throne, the king died.

(The KING dies, dropping his crown. The QUEEN and the PRINCE struggle over the crown. The QUEEN takes the crown and places it on her head.)

The prince, meanwhile, had fallen in love.

(The FARMER'S DAUGHTER appears.)

CONOR   I knew it! These kinds of stories always have stupid princes falling in love. I thought this was going to be good.

(The MONSTER hoists CONOR into the air.)

Arrggghhh!

MONSTER   Silence! *(Beat)* As I was saying, the prince had fallen in love – with a humble farmer's daughter.

(The PRINCE goes to the FARMER'S DAUGHTER.)

The queen, however, had other plans – for the prince to marry her instead!

(The QUEEN approaches the PRINCE, seductively.)

CONOR   That's disgusting. She was his grandmother!

MONSTER   Step-grandmother – not related by blood.

CONOR   That's just wrong.

MONSTER   The prince said he would rather die than marry the queen, so he ran from the kingdom with his beloved.

(The PRINCE and the FARMER'S DAUGHTER run away together. They arrive at the foot of a large yew tree.)

They stopped only at dawn in the shade of a giant yew tree.

CONOR   And that was you?!

MONSTER   It was me.

(The PRINCE and the FARMER'S DAUGHTER make love under the tree, then sleep.)

They slept through the day in the shadows of my branches.

CONOR   They're not doing much sleeping.

(Beat)

MONSTER   Until night fell once again.

(The PRINCE wakes up.)

PRINCE   Arise, my beloved, for we ride to the day where we
                 shall be man and wife.

(The PRINCE realizes that the FARMER'S DAUGHTER is dead.)

CONOR   Blood?!

(The PRINCE sees blood on his hands. He sees a knife and picks it up.)

PRINCE   The queen! The queen is responsible for this
                 treachery!

MONSTER   If the villagers found him they would call him a
                 murderer and put him to death for his crime.

CONOR   And the queen would be able to rule unchallenged.
                 I hope this story ends with you ripping her head off.

MONSTER   There was nowhere for the prince to run. He lifted
                 his head to the great tree and spoke.

CONOR   What did he say?

MONSTER   He said enough to bring me walking.

(A group of VILLAGERS approach.)

PRINCE   *(To VILLAGERS)* The queen has murdered my bride!
                 The queen must be stopped!

MONSTER   It took very little for the villagers to see the obvious
                 truth. They stormed the castle and dragged the
                 queen to the stake to burn her alive.

CONOR   Good. She deserved it. *(Beat)* I don't suppose you
                 can help me with my grandma? I mean, I don't want
                 to burn her alive or anything, but maybe just—

MONSTER   The story is not yet finished.

CONOR   But the queen was overthrown.

MONSTER	She was. But not by me.
CONOR	You said you made sure she was never seen again.
MONSTER	And so I did. When the villagers lit the flames, I reached in and saved her.
CONOR	What?

(The QUEEN crosses the space.)

MONSTER	I took her far away, where the villagers would never find her.
CONOR	How could you possibly save a murderer?
MONSTER	I never said she killed the farmer's daughter. I only said that the prince said it was so.
CONOR	Who killed her then?

(The story rewinds so the MONSTER can show what really happened. The PRINCE and FARMER'S DAUGHTER sleep at the base of the tree again.)

MONSTER   Watch. And witness what really happened. *(Beat)* After their coupling, the prince remained awake.

(The PRINCE looks at the sleeping FARMER'S DAUGHTER. He takes out a knife and stabs the FARMER'S DAUGHTER.)

CONOR   No!

(The FARMER'S DAUGHTER dies.)

You said he was surprised when she didn't wake up!

MONSTER   That was all a pantomime, acted out by the prince for anyone watching. But it was also for himself – sometimes people need to lie to themselves most of all.

CONOR	You said he asked for your help, and that you gave it!
MONSTER	I only said he told me enough to bring me walking.
CONOR	What did he tell you?

MONSTER   He told me that he had done it for the good of the kingdom. That the new queen was a witch, and that he needed the fury of the villagers to help topple her. The death of the farmer's daughter saw to that. When he said that the queen had murdered his bride, he believed, in his own way, that it was actually true.

CONOR   That's a load of crap! The people were behind him anyway.

MONSTER   The reason I came walking – was for the queen, not the prince.

CONOR   Did he ever get caught? Did they punish him?

MONSTER   He became a much-loved king, who ruled happily until the end of his long days.

(The PRINCE exits.)

CONOR   So the good prince was a murderer and the evil queen wasn't a witch after all. Is that supposed to be the lesson of all this – that I should be nice to Grandma?!

MONSTER   You think I have come walking out of time and earth itself to teach you a lesson in niceness?

CONOR   Yeah, all right.

MONSTER   The queen could have been a witch – and may even have been on her way to great evil, who's to say?

CONOR   Why did you save her, then?

MONSTER   Because she was not a murderer.

CONOR   I don't understand. Who's the good guy here?

MONSTER   There is not always a good guy. Nor is there always a bad one. Most people are somewhere in-between.

CONOR   That's a terrible story.

MONSTER   It's a true story.

CONOR	And a cheat.
MONSTER	Many things that are true feel like a cheat. Kingdoms get the princes they deserve, farmers' daughters die and sometimes witches merit saving. Quite often, actually – you'd be surprised.
CONOR	So how is that supposed to save me from Grandma?
MONSTER	It's not her you need saving from.

(The MONSTER disappears.)

11.
UNDERSTANDING

(Wednesday afternoon. School playground.)

(LILY enters, collecting her rucksack.)

LILY	*(To CONOR)* I forgive you.
CONOR	For what?
LILY	I forgive you for getting me into trouble, stupid.
CONOR	You got yourself into trouble. You're the one who punched Anton.
LILY	I forgive you for lying.

(Pause)

Well, aren't you going to say you're sorry back?

CONOR	No.
LILY	Why not?
CONOR	Because I'm not sorry.
LILY	Conor…
CONOR	I'm not sorry, and I don't forgive you.

(Beat)

LILY   My mum said we need to make allowances for you. Because of what you're going through.

CONOR   Your mum doesn't know anything. And neither do you.

(ANTON and SULLY enter.)

SULLY   Oi, oi, O'Malley!

ANTON   All right.

(CONOR goes to exit. SULLY blocks his way. LILY stands apart, watching.)

SULLY   *(To CONOR)* Where you off?

CONOR   Home.

ANTON   Go on then.

(CONOR tries again, but SULLY stops him.)

SULLY   It's not that way, is it?

(CONOR tries another way, but ANTON stops him, half-heartedly.)

ANTON   I think it's this way.

(SULLY and ANTON continue to block CONOR's path. SULLY pushes CONOR to the floor.)

(LILY goes to exit.)

(CONOR stays on the floor.)

SULLY   Oh, Super Poodle?! You not gonna help him out today?!

(LILY exits.)

   (Reacting to LILY abandoning CONOR) Owww! *(To CONOR)* Get up then, Bambi.

(SULLY grabs hold of CONOR, pulling him to his feet.)

(HARRY enters.)

HARRY   Hey, what's going on?! Nobody touches O'Malley
                  except for me.

SULLY   But we were—

HARRY   Err, sorry, but did I ask for your opinion? *(Beat)* Yeh,
                  so shush, schtum, yeh?! *(Beat)* 'Cos O'Malley and I
                  have an unwritten rule, don't we, O'Malley? I'm the
                  only one who touches you, isn't that right?

(HARRY goes to hit CONOR, but stops short. CONOR moves to dodge the attack.)

                  Ha, ha! You all right Flinchy McFlincherson?!

(HARRY pretends to hit CONOR again, but CONOR doesn't flinch. HARRY tries again and again, but CONOR does not respond.)

                  Oh, you're getting brave now, are ya?! Do you want me
                  to give you something to be brave about? Come on!

(CONOR looks at HARRY.)

(MISS GODFREY enters.)

MISS GODFREY   Year Eight! Home-time was ten minutes ago! What
                  do you think you're still doing out here?

HARRY   Sorry, Miss. We were talking about Mr Marl's
                  life writing homework. 'Cos you see, Miss, it's
                  been really tough for Anton with the passing of his
                  hamster, and Conor here was just really worried
                  about him.

MISS GODFREY   That sounds entirely plausible, thank you, Harry.
                  Everybody here is on first warning. One more
                  problem this week, and that's detention, for all of you.

ANTON   What for?!

SULLY   We didn't do nothing!

HARRY   Yes, Miss. Miss, that hamster was like a brother
                  to him.

MISS GODFREY   That's quite enough, Harry.

(HARRY, SULLY and ANTON exit.)

(CONOR follows but is stopped by MISS GODFREY.)

A moment please, Conor.

(CONOR turns but doesn't look at MISS GODFREY.)

Are you sure everything's all right between you and those three?

CONOR   Yes, Miss.

MISS GODFREY   Because I'm not blind to the way Harry works, you know. A bully with top marks and charisma is still a bully. He'll probably end up Prime Minister one day, God help us all.

(Pause)

I can't imagine what you must be going through – but if you ever need to talk, my door is always open.

CONOR   I'm fine, Miss. I'm not going through anything.

MISS GODFREY   All right. Forget about the first warning. Get yourself home.

(MISS GODFREY exits.)

12.
LITTLE TALK

(Friday afternoon. The hallway of CONOR's house.)

(GRANDMA enters, carrying MUM's bags for the hospital. MUM sits in the kitchen.)

GRANDMA   Ah, we need to have a talk.

CONOR   What's wrong?

(Beat)

GRANDMA   I'm taking your mother back into hospital. You're going to come and stay with me for a few days. You'll need to pack a bag.

CONOR   What's wrong with her?

(Beat)

GRANDMA   There's a lot of pain. Much more than there should be.

CONOR   She's got medicine for her pain.

(GRANDMA claps her hands together, sharply.)

GRANDMA   It's not working, Conor. It is not working.

CONOR   What's not working?

(GRANDMA taps her hands together, softly.)

GRANDMA   Your mother is in the kitchen – she wants to speak to you before she leaves.

CONOR   But—

GRANDMA   Your father's flying in from America on Sunday.

CONOR   Dad's coming?! Why is Dad coming?

GRANDMA   I have to bring the car round.

CONOR   But he hasn't been in ages!

GRANDMA   Get yourself some supper. I know you can do that. I'll collect you on my way home from the hospital later. Please be ready.

(GRANDMA exits.)

MUM   Con?

(CONOR goes into the kitchen.)

Hey...

CONOR   What's the matter? Why are you going back to hospital? *(Beat)* What's wrong?

MUM   I'm going to be OK. I really am.

CONOR	Are you?
MUM	Conor, we've been here before, don't worry. I've felt really bad, and I've gone in, and they've taken care of it. That's what'll happen this time.
CONOR	Why is Dad coming?
MUM	What do you mean? It'll be great for you to see him.
CONOR	Grandma doesn't seem too happy.
MUM	Well, you know how she feels about your dad. Don't listen to her.

(Beat)

CONOR	There's something else, isn't there?

(Beat)

MUM	Conor, listen … this latest treatment's not doing what it's supposed to do. And all that means is they're going to have to adjust it, try something else.
CONOR	That's it?
MUM	That's it. There's lots more they can do. It's normal. Don't worry.
CONOR	You're sure?
MUM	I'm sure.
CONOR	Because … you could tell me, you know.
MUM	Conor…

(MUM goes to CONOR and hugs him.)

(MUM turns to the window and looks out, encouraging CONOR to do the same.)

	Look, you see that—
CONOR	Yes, Mum, it's a yew tree – you've told me a hundred times.

MUM   Keep an eye on it for me, won't you? Make sure it's
               there when I get back.

CONOR   I will.

*(MUM kisses CONOR on the forehead, then puts on her coat, picks up her
bag and exits.)*

13.
GRANDMA'S HOUSE

(Monday afternoon. GRANDMA's house.)

*(GRANDMA is in the sitting room. She goes to a grandfather clock,
adjusts the time and winds the mechanism.)*

(CONOR watches from the doorway, unseen by GRANDMA.)

*(GRANDMA sets the pendulum swinging, watches the clock for a moment,
then turns to see CONOR watching her.)*

GRANDMA   *(Surprised)* Oh … yes… I was just winding the clock.

CONOR   Right.

*(GRANDMA goes to leave the sitting room, ushering CONOR away from
the doorway.)*

GRANDMA   Well … erm … yes. That clock belonged to your
               great-grandmother, you know.

CONOR   I know.

GRANDMA   It was made in 1831 by Mark Bartley, clockmaker
               of Bristol. And to our knowledge, has been in the
               family ever since. Isn't that marvellous?

(GRANDMA goes into the kitchen. CONOR follows.)

               Remember, you're not allowed in the sitting room
               while I'm not here. It is strictly out of bounds, all
               right?

CONOR   Yes, Grandma.

GRANDMA   Thank you. Because that's important to me. *(Beat)*
           Now, your father will be here soon.

CONOR   Does he know where you live?

GRANDMA   I've sent him the address. *(Beat)* Now pick up your
           rucksack please – no need for him to think I'm
           keeping you in a pigsty.

CONOR   Not much chance of that.

GRANDMA   No, no chance at all, I don't like pigsties. *(Beat)*
           Right, I'm off to see your mum.

(GRANDMA prepares to leave the house.)

           Oh Conor, your father may not notice how tired
           your mum gets, OK? So, we're going to have to
           work together to make sure he doesn't overstay his
           welcome. Not that that's ever been a problem. *(Beat)*
           Now be good, and I'll see you at the hospital later.

(GRANDMA ruffles CONOR's hair, then goes to exit.)

           Gosh, you're so tall these days.

(GRANDMA exits.)

*(CONOR is alone again. He goes to the sitting room, but the
doorbell rings.)*

(CONOR goes to the front door.)

(DAD enters.)

CONOR   Dad!

DAD   Hey, Con.

(CONOR and DAD hug.)

14.
CHAMP

(Monday afternoon. A park.)

(CONOR and DAD walk together, eating takeaway chips.)

CONOR   She looked all right, didn't she?

DAD   Yeah … all things considered, I suppose she did.

CONOR   And the doctor said she might be able to come home soon.

DAD   Well, that'd be nice, wouldn't it?

CONOR   It will.

(CONOR and DAD sit down on the floor to eat their chips.)

DAD   So how are you hanging in there, champ?

CONOR   Champ?

DAD   Sorry. Americans talk completely differently.

CONOR   Your voice sounds funnier every time I talk to you.

DAD   *(Cod American accent)* Well, gee, next time you see me I'll be talking like—

CONOR   Dad!

DAD   It's good to see you.

   (Pause)

               Con, your mum… *(Beat)* She's a fighter, isn't she?

(CONOR shrugs.)

               You doing OK?

CONOR   That's like the eight hundredth time you've asked me since you got here! I'm fine.

DAD   Sorry.

CONOR   Mum's on this new medicine. I know she looks bad,
             but she's looked bad before. Why is everyone acting
             like—

DAD   No, you're right. But you're going to need to be
             brave – real brave.

CONOR   You talk like American television.

(Pause)

DAD   Your sister's doing well.

CONOR   Half-sister.

DAD   She's walking now ... toddling about all over the
             place. I can't wait for you to meet her. You'll have to
             come visit. Maybe this Christmas.

CONOR   What about Mum?

DAD   I've talked to your grandma – she seemed to think it
             was a good idea, just as long as we get you back for
             the start of the new school term.

CONOR   So it'd just be a visit then?

DAD   As opposed to—? *(Beat)* Con.

CONOR   There's a tree that's been visiting me. It comes to the
             house at night and tells me stories.

DAD   What?

CONOR   I thought it was a dream at first, but then I found
             these berries in my shoes, so I hid them so no one
             will find out.

DAD   Conor—

CONOR   It hasn't come to Grandma's house yet. I think she
             might live too far away—

DAD   What are you—?

CONOR	But why should it matter if it's all a dream? Why wouldn't a dream be able to walk across town? Not if it's as old as the earth and as big as the world—
DAD	Conor, stop—
CONOR	I don't want to live at Grandma's house! Why can't I come and live with you? Why can't I come to America?

(Pause)

Grandma's house is an old lady house.

(Beat)

DAD	I'm going to tell her you called her an old lady.
CONOR	You can't touch anything or sit anywhere. You can't leave a mess for even two seconds. And she's only got the internet in her office and I'm not even allowed in there.
DAD	We can talk to her about that stuff. We can make you more comfortable there.
CONOR	I don't want to be comfortable there! I want my own room in my own house.
DAD	You wouldn't have that in America, Conor. We live in a small apartment. Your grandma's got more money, more space than we have. And your whole life is here, isn't it? Your friends, your school, everything. It'd be unfair to take you away from all of that.
CONOR	Unfair to who?
DAD	This is what I meant … about needing to be brave.
CONOR	As if that means anything.
DAD	I wish things were different.
CONOR	Do you?

DAD   Of course I do. I know it seems unfair... But it's for the best, you'll see.

CONOR   Can we stop talking about this now?

DAD   Of course we can, buddy.

CONOR   Buddy?

(CONOR goes to exit.)

DAD   Sorry.

(DAD chases after CONOR.)

15.
AMERICANS DON'T GET MUCH HOLIDAY

(Monday evening, just before 10 p.m. Outside GRANDMA's house.)

(CONOR and DAD arrive at GRANDMA's front door.)

DAD   Doesn't look like your grandma's home yet.

CONOR   She sometimes stays late at the hospital. The nurses let her sleep in a chair.

DAD   She might not like me, Con, but it doesn't mean she's a bad person.

CONOR   How long are you here for?

DAD   Just a few days, I'm afraid.

CONOR   That's all?

DAD   Americans don't get much holiday.

CONOR   You're not American.

DAD   I live there now.

(Beat)

CONOR   Why did you come then? Why bother coming at all?

DAD   I came because your mum asked me to.

(Pause)

> Do you want me to come in and wait with you till she gets home?

CONOR   I'm fine on my own.

DAD   Conor...

(CONOR goes into GRANDMA's house.)

(DAD exits.)

(CONOR goes to the sitting room and steps inside. He watches the clock. The clock strikes ten o'clock.)

(CONOR goes to the clock and breaks the pendulum.)

(CONOR forces the hour hand of the clock to 12.)

ENSEMBLE   12.

(CONOR forces the minute hand of the clock to 7 minutes past the hour.)

> 07.

(The MONSTER enters.)

MONSTER   As destruction goes this is all remarkably pitiful. It is the kind of destruction I would expect from a boy.

CONOR   What are you doing here?

MONSTER   I have come to tell you the second tale.

CONOR   Is it going to be as bad as the last one?

MONSTER   It ends in proper destruction, if that's what you mean.

CONOR   Is it another cheating story? Does it sound like it's going to be one way and then it's a total other?

MONSTER   No. It is about a man who thought only of himself. And he gets punished very badly indeed.

CONOR   I'm listening.

16.
THE SECOND TALE/DESTRUCTION

(The ENSEMBLE transform the space.)

MONSTER   One hundred and fifty years ago this country had become a place of industry. *(Beat)* Villages grew into towns, towns into cities. Trees fell, fields were upended, rivers blackened. The sky choked on smoke and ash. And so did the people. *(Beat)* But there was still green, if you knew where to look.

(Pause)

     There was a man. His name was not important. The villagers only ever called him the Apothecary.

(The APOTHECARY emerges from the ENSEMBLE and picks berries and leaves. The ENSEMBLE become VILLAGERS.)

CONOR   What's an apothecary?

MONSTER   It's an old-fashioned name for a chemist.

CONOR   Why didn't you just say that then?

MONSTER   Apothecaries dealt in the old ways of medicine – of ancient concoctions brewed from berries and leaves.

CONOR   Dad's new wife does that – she owns a shop that sells crystals.

(The APOTHECARY and the VILLAGERS turn on CONOR.)

MONSTER   It is not remotely the same. *(Beat)* Many a day the Apothecary searched for herbs and barks, but as the cities sprawled, the green continued to disappear. The Apothecary grew bitter, and often charged his patients more than they could afford to pay. *(Beat)* He was a greedy man.

(The PARSON emerges from the ENSEMBLE.)

In the village there also lived a parson. He was an enlightened man, a man of deep faith. *(Beat)* The parson also had two daughters. They were the light of his life.

(The PARSON'S DAUGHTERS emerge from the ENSEMBLE.)

On the parsonage grounds there also grew...

(A large yew tree appears.)

CONOR   A yew tree.

MONSTER   And a very handsome tree it was.

CONOR   Even if you do say so yourself.

(The PARSON and the PARSON'S DAUGHTERS sit under the tree.)

MONSTER   Now, the Apothecary wanted the parson's yew tree very badly.

CONOR   Why?

MONSTER   It is the most important of all the healing trees.

CONOR   You're making that up!

MONSTER   It had stood in the church grounds for many hundreds of years. But in order to harvest medicine from the tree, the Apothecary would have had to cut it down.

(The APOTHECARY approaches the tree, carrying an axe.)

(SONG: "Please Give Me")

APOTHECARY *Give me, give me, oh give me your tree,*
           The power to heal lies within the leaves,
           The ancient yew that stands in your ground
           I must, I must, I must cut it down.

           The roots are my scripture, the bark is my cross,
           I have the money to cover the cost.

MONSTER   But the parson would not give up the tree. Instead he preached against the Apothecary's use of old and superstitious ways. *(Beat)* The Apothecary went back to the parson and begged. He begged…

(The APOTHECARY writes a letter.)

APOTHECARY *Give me.*

MONSTER Again.

APOTHECARY *Give me.*

MONSTER Again.

APOTHECARY *Oh give me your tree.*

(The letter is delivered to the PARSON.)

MONSTER The parson replied.

APOTHECARY *No.*

MONSTER Again.

APOTHECARY *No.*

MONSTER Again.

(The PARSON reads the letter, then screws it up and throws it on the ground.)

APOTHECARY *You can't take my tree.*

MONSTER So the Apothecary's business shrank and he grew more bitter than ever.

(The APOTHECARY is broken.)

(The PARSON'S DAUGHTERS play around the yew tree. The PARSON watches them.)

Then one day a disease swept the country, and the parson's daughters fell sick.

(The PARSON'S DAUGHTERS stop playing and grow sick.)

APOTHECARY *Ooooo.*
Ohhhh.

MONSTER   No prayer, no modern medicine could heal them.
               There was nothing the parson could do. *(Beat)* He
               felt he had no other choice.

PARSON   *I'll give you, I'll give you, I'll give you my tree.*
               I will give up all that I believe.
               I'll tear up my scriptures, and I'll burn my cross,
               I'll give up my god if you'll stop my loss.

   (The PARSON crawls towards the APOTHECARY.)

               My girls will die if you don't help me.
               O please save, o please save, my daughters of Eve.

   (The PARSON kneels at the APOTHECARY's feet, offering him up an axe.)

APOTHECARY   You'll give me the tree? You'd give up everything
               you believe in?

PARSON   If it will save my daughters.

APOTHECARY   Then there is nothing I can do to help you.

   (The APOTHECARY refuses the axe and exits.)

CONOR   What?!

MONSTER   That very night, both of the parson's daughters died.

CONOR   What?!

MONSTER   And that very night, I came walking.

CONOR   Good! That stupid git deserves all the punishment
               he gets.

MONSTER   I thought so too. *(Beat)* It was shortly after
               midnight that I tore the parson's home from its very
               foundations.

CONOR   The parson?

MONSTER   I knocked down every wall of his house and flung his
               roof into the dell below.

   *(We hear the sound of destruction, followed by "Adagio of Spartacus and
   Phrygia" by Aram Khachaturian.)*

(The ENSEMBLE begin to destroy the parsonage.)

CONOR   What are you doing? The Apothecary is the bad
             guy!

MONSTER   He was certainly bad-tempered and greedy. But he
             was still a healer.

CONOR   He refused to help the parson's daughters! And they
             died!

MONSTER   The parson was willing to throw aside every belief
             he had in order to save his daughters.

CONOR   So would anyone!

MONSTER   Belief is half of all healing. The parson – what was
             he? A man of faith without faith.

(The MONSTER further destroys the parsonage.)

             So tell me, Conor O'Malley, would you like to join
             in?

CONOR   Join in?

MONSTER   It is most satisfying, I assure you.

CONOR   What shall I do?

(The MONSTER laughs.)

MONSTER   Anything you feel!

(The MONSTER exits.)

("Adagio of Spartacus and Phrygia" builds to its climax.)

*(CONOR explodes into a tantrum and further destroys the parsonage.
However, he is actually wrecking GRANDMA's sitting room.)*

(CONOR stops wrecking. The music suddenly stops.)

             (From off, half-voice) Now that is how destruction is
             properly done.

(CONOR surveys the damage.)

CONOR   Oh my God. Oh my God! *(Shouting off to MONSTER)* What have you done!?

(CONOR turns to the MONSTER but it has gone.)

(CONOR picks up the broken pendulum, realizing what he has done.)

(GRANDMA enters carrying a handbag and sees the destruction. She drops her handbag.)

(GRANDMA notices CONOR. She groans a painful sound. CONOR is petrified.)

           Grandma?

(GRANDMA screams.)

(GRANDMA approaches CONOR as though she is going to hurt him. Instead she passes him and picks up the only unbroken item left in the room. GRANDMA throws the item across the room, breaking it into pieces.)

(GRANDMA exits, leaving CONOR standing amongst the destruction.)

(Blackout.)

END OF ACT ONE

ACT TWO

17.
THE NIGHTMARE (2)

(CONOR and the ENSEMBLE enter.)

(The nightmare.)

(The ENSEMBLE sit down.)

18.
THE MORNING AFTER

(Tuesday morning. GRANDMA's house.)

(DAD enters and looks at CONOR, apprehensively.)

(DAD picks up a box of cornflakes.)

DAD   *(To CONOR)* Cornflakes?

(CONOR sits down.)

(DAD takes a bowl and pours cornflakes and milk into it.)

Where does your grandma keep the spoons?

(DAD finds a spoon, then hands CONOR his breakfast.)

(CONOR eats, slowly.)

(Long pause)

That was quite a mess you made last night.

(Pause)

Your grandma called me this morning – very,
very early. Your mum's taken a turn. *(Beat)* Your

	grandma's at the hospital now, talking to the doctors. I'm going to drop you off at school—
CONOR	School?! I don't want to go to school. I want to see my mum!
DAD	It's the best place for you, Con.
CONOR	No it's not. I need to go to the hospital.
DAD	I'll pick you up after school and take you straight there.
CONOR	I want to see her now.
DAD	Conor!
CONOR	You don't get to just turn up out of the blue and tell me what to do.
DAD	It's for your mum – she needs to rest.
CONOR	So why are you going? Why is Grandma there?
DAD	Look, I'll pick you up sooner if I need to.

(Pause)

Remember what I said about needing to be brave? Well, that's what you've got to do. *(Beat)* I can see how much this is upsetting you. So can your grandma.

(Beat)

| CONOR | I didn't mean to. I don't know what happened. |
| DAD | It's OK. |

(Beat)

CONOR	It's *OK*?
DAD	Don't worry about it.
CONOR	What do you mean, it's OK?
DAD	Worse things happen at sea.

CONOR   What the hell does that mean?!

DAD   Conor! *(Beat)* Look, we're going to pretend like none
               of this ever happened. There are other things going
               on right now.

CONOR   Other things like Mum?

DAD   Finish your breakfast.

CONOR   You're not even going to punish me?

DAD   What would be the point, Con? What could possibly
               be the point?

(DAD exits.)

(CONOR stands alone.)

19.
WHAT DO YOU WANT?

(Tuesday afternoon. The school playground.)

*(HARRY, SULLY and ANTON enter. HARRY watches CONOR from
a distance.)*

SULLY   Here he is!

ANTON   Hi, Conor.

SULLY   Don't say hi, Anton! *(To CONOR)* Come on then,
               O'Malley, let's have ya!

(SULLY tips the contents of CONOR's rucksack on the floor.)

               (To ANTON) Hey, watch this.

(SULLY puts the rucksack over CONOR's head.)

               Give us a smile, Con!

(CONOR removes the rucksack from his head.)

(HARRY approaches CONOR, slowly.)

               Here we go.

(HARRY gathers the contents of CONOR's rucksack and hands them back to CONOR.)

(HARRY and CONOR stare at each other.)

CONOR   What are you waiting for?

SULLY   Yeah, what are you waiting for?

ANTON   Hit him.

HARRY   What am I waiting for, O'Malley? Do you think you can tell me what it is I'm waiting for?

(Beat)

CONOR   *(Throwing contents of rucksack to the floor)* Just do it!

(Beat)

HARRY   Do what, O'Malley?

SULLY   I think he wants you to punch him in the face.

ANTON   He wants you to kick his arse.

HARRY   Is that right?! Is that really what you want?

(HARRY stands close to CONOR, threateningly. The school bell rings.)

               I guess we'll never find out what it is that O'Malley wants.

(ANTON and SULLY exit.)

(CONOR repacks his rucksack.)

(HARRY exits, still watching CONOR.)

(CONOR stands alone.)

20.
YEW TREES

(Tuesday evening. The hospital.)

(The ENSEMBLE move MUM into a chair and prepare an intravenous drip in her arm. GRANDMA stands behind her, tying her headscarf.)

(CONOR enters, uneasily.)

MUM   Hi, Con!

(GRANDMA notices CONOR.)

GRANDMA   *(To MUM)* I'll just be out here.

(GRANDMA exits, not looking at CONOR.)

MUM   How are you? Sorry, I must look a fright.

CONOR   No, you don't.

MUM   Did you have a good time with your dad?

CONOR   He bought me chips and kept calling me buddy.

MUM   *(Laughing)* Buddy!

CONOR   And champ.

MUM   *(Still laughing)* Champ…

　　　(Beat)

CONOR   Dad said you'd taken a turn.

MUM   Well, he shouldn't have said that. *(Beat)* I'm fine, sweetheart. Just … a couple of things they've tried haven't worked like they wanted them to. And they've not worked a lot sooner than they were hoping they wouldn't. If that makes any sense?

(CONOR shakes his head, slightly.)

　　　　　　　　 No, not to me either really. But, there's one more thing they're going to try. It's a medicine that's had some good results.

CONOR   Why didn't they try it before?

MUM   I don't know – they probably just didn't want to use it too soon.

CONOR   Does that mean it's too late?

MUM   No! No, Con, don't think that! It's not too late. It's never too late.

CONOR   Are you sure?

MUM   I believe every word I say. *(Beat)* And this is the amazing thing – you know the yew tree on the hill behind our house – well, if you can believe it – this drug is actually made from yew trees!

CONOR   Yew trees?!

(The MONSTER enters.)

MUM   Yes! I read about it way back, when this all started. I mean, I hoped it would never get this far...

(The MONSTER approaches MUM, slowly.)

           But it just seems incredible that all this time we could see this yew tree from our house. And that this tree could be the very thing that heals me.

(The MONSTER puts its hands on MUM's shoulders.)

           The green things of this world are just wondrous, aren't they? We work so hard to get rid of them... And sometimes they're the very thing that saves us.

CONOR   Is it going to save you?

MUM   I believe so.

(CONOR daydreams.)

(The MONSTER takes MUM and dances with her.)

(CONOR drifts into the air, euphoric.)

CONOR   Belief is half of all healing.

21.
COULD IT BE?

(Later Tuesday evening. The hospital.)

(DAD and GRANDMA enter, arguing. DAD is carrying two cups from a vending machine.)

DAD   I understand exactly what you're saying—

GRANDMA   Do you? Because I don't think you do.

DAD   What else do you want from me, Yvonne? I am doing everything—

GRANDMA   You need to speak to him.

DAD   I'm going to speak to him.

GRANDMA   How can you? How can you possibly—?

(DAD and GRANDMA look at CONOR, then at each other.)

CONOR   What's going on?

(GRANDMA exits.)

(CONOR and DAD call a lift and wait for it.)

DAD   I got you a hot chocolate.

(DAD offers CONOR one of the cups. CONOR ignores it.)

            Your grandma's mad at me. Nothing new there.

CONOR   Why?

DAD   I've got some bad news, Conor. I have to fly back to America tonight.

CONOR   Tonight? Why?

DAD   The baby's sick.

CONOR   Oh… What's wrong with her?

DAD	Probably nothing serious, but Stephanie's gone a bit crazy and taken her into hospital. She wants me home right away.
CONOR	And you're going?
DAD	I am. But I'll be back – a week on Sunday. So it's not even two weeks.

(The lift arrives. CONOR and DAD get in.)

CONOR	Two weeks – that's OK. Mum's on this new medicine which is going to make her better. So by the time you get back—
DAD	Conor, this new medicine your mum's taking—
CONOR	It's going to make her well.
DAD	No, it probably isn't.
CONOR	Yes, it is.
DAD	It's a last-ditch effort… Things have moved so fast. I'm sorry.
CONOR	It'll heal her, I know it will.
DAD	The other reason your grandma's mad at me is because she doesn't think me or your mum have been honest enough with you about what's really happening.
CONOR	What does Grandma know about it?
DAD	Conor, your mum—
CONOR	She's going to be OK. This new medicine is the secret. It's the whole reason why. I'm telling you, I know.
DAD	Reason for what?
CONOR	So you just go back to America … and go back to your other family, and we'll be fine here without you. Because this is going to work.

DAD   Conor, no—

(The lift stops.)

CONOR   Yes, it is, it's going to work.

(CONOR gets out of the lift. DAD follows.)

DAD   This is too much. *(Beat)* Look, I'm going to drop
                  you off at your grandma's now, but I'll be back a
                  week on Sunday, all right?

CONOR   How long will you stay?

DAD   For as long as I can.

CONOR   And then you'll go back…

DAD   I have to. I've got—

CONOR   Another family there.

DAD   Con—

(DAD exits.)

(CONOR stands alone.)

22.
NO TALE

(Tuesday night. GRANDMA's house.)

(CONOR picks up a carriage clock and carries it around the room, staring at it intently. The clock turns to 12.07.)

ENSEMBLE   12.07.

CONOR   Where are you?!

(The MONSTER appears.)

MONSTER   I am here.

CONOR   Can you heal her?

MONSTER   The yew tree is a healing tree.

CONOR   That's not really an answer. *(Beat)* Can you heal her?

MONSTER   It is not up to me.

CONOR   Why not? You tear down houses and rescue witches. You say you have the power to heal.

MONSTER   If your mother can be healed, then the yew tree will do it.

CONOR   Is that a yes?

MONSTER   You still don't know why you have called me, do you, Conor O'Malley?

CONOR   I didn't call you. And if I did, it was obviously for my mum.

MONSTER   Was it?

CONOR   Well, it wasn't just to hear terrible stories that make no sense.

MONSTER   Are you forgetting your grandmother's sitting room?

(The MONSTER laughs.)

CONOR   I'm being serious.

MONSTER   So am I. *(Beat)* You are not yet ready for the third tale. But you will be soon. And after that, you will tell me *your* story, Conor O'Malley. You will tell me the truth. And you know of what I speak.

(CONOR is suddenly thrust into the nightmare.)

CONOR   No! No! Not this! That's not my truth. That's just a nightmare.

(The nightmare stops.)

MONSTER   Nevertheless, that is what will happen after the third tale.

CONOR   Great – another story when there are more important things going on.

MONSTER	Stories are important – if they carry the truth. *(Beat)* Look for me soon.
CONOR	I want to know what's going to happen with my mum.
MONSTER	Do you not know already?
CONOR	You said you were a tree of healing. Well, I need you to heal!
MONSTER	And so I shall.

(The MONSTER exits.)

(CONOR is left alone.)

23.
WHEN IS SHE GOING TO COME HOME?

(Wednesday morning. GRANDMA's car.)

(GRANDMA is driving CONOR to school.)

CONOR	I want to go to the hospital too. I don't want to go to school today.

(Long pause)

How was Mum last night?

(Pause)

GRANDMA	Much the same.
CONOR	Is the new medicine working?

(Pause)

GRANDMA	It's too soon to tell.

(Long pause)

CONOR	When is she going to come home?

(Very long pause)

GRANDMA	I'll pick you up after school.

(CONOR gets out of the car. GRANDMA exits.)

(CONOR is left alone.)

24.
THE THIRD TALE

(Wednesday lunchtime. School canteen.)

SULLY   *(From off)* Conor O'Malley!

(SULLY and ANTON enter. SULLY goes to CONOR and empties a half-full bottle of cola over him.)

ANTON   Why would you do that?

SULLY   It looks like he's wet himself.

ANTON   But why would you do that?

SULLY   'Cos it's funny, Anton! Why are you always sticking up for him?!

(HARRY enters and circles CONOR, menacingly.)

HARRY   I think I've worked you out, O'Malley. I think I know what it is you're asking for.

SULLY   *(To ANTON)* He's gonna get it now.

(HARRY faces up to CONOR.)

HARRY   Here is the hardest hit of all, O'Malley. Here is the very worst thing I can do to you.

(HARRY holds out his hand for CONOR to shake. CONOR looks at HARRY, then shakes his hand.)

                   (Shaking hands) Goodbye, O'Malley. I no longer see you.

(HARRY drops CONOR's hand and walks away.)

(SULLY and ANTON exit, dumbfounded.)

(The clock turns to 12.07.)

CONOR   12.07.

(The MONSTER enters.)

MONSTER   It is time for the third tale.

(The MONSTER makes his way towards CONOR, slowly.)

There was once an invisible man who had grown
tired of being unseen. It was not that he was actually
invisible. It was that people had become used to not
seeing him.

(The MONSTER stands behind CONOR.)

(CONOR fixes his eyes on HARRY.)

CONOR   Hey!

MONSTER   And if no one sees you, are you really there at all?

CONOR   Hey!

MONSTER   Then one day the invisible man decided, "I will
make them see me."

CONOR   How? How did the man do it?

MONSTER   He called for a monster.

*(The MONSTER holds CONOR by the head and pulls him to his feet.
CONOR stands with the MONSTER, his eyes still fixed on HARRY.)*

CONOR &
MONSTER   Harry!

(HARRY is suddenly thrown across the space and onto the floor.)

HARRY   What do you think you're playing at, O'Malley?

CONOR &
MONSTER   You don't see me? You don't see me?!

HARRY   *(Standing)* No, I don't! And guess what? No one here
does! *(Beat)* You think this scares me? You think
I'm ever going to be afraid of you? *(Beat)* Conor
O'Malley, who everyone feels sorry for because of his

mum, who swans around like he's so different, like no one knows he's suffering. *(Beat)* Conor O'Malley, who wants to be punished. Conor O'Malley, who needs to be punished. Why is that, O'Malley? What messed-up secrets do you hide that are so terrible?

CONOR &
MONSTER   You shut up!

HARRY   Do you know what I see when I look at you, O'Malley?

(CONOR clenches his fists.)

               I see nothing.

CONOR   *(To the MONSTER, eyes still fixed on HARRY)* What did you do to help the invisible man?

MONSTER   I made them see.

(The MONSTER laughs.)

(The ENSEMBLE transform the space.)

(HARRY is thrown, like a rag-doll, around the space.)

CONOR   Never invisible again. Never invisible again!

CONOR &
MONSTER   Never invisible again! Never invisible again!

CONOR   Never invisible again!

(HARRY lies motionless on the floor. CONOR stands over him, exhausted.)

MONSTER   *(Half-voice)* But there are harder things than being invisible.

(The MONSTER and the ENSEMBLE exit.)

25.
PUNISHMENT

(Wednesday afternoon. MISS GODFREY's office.)

(MISS GODFREY enters. CONOR looks at the ground.)

MISS GODFREY   I don't even know what to say. What can I possibly say to you, Conor? You broke his arm, his nose... Knocked out his teeth! His parents are threatening to sue the school *and* file charges against you.

(CONOR looks up.)

They were very upset. And I don't blame them. I can't even make sense of what actually happened myself. *(Beat)* I explained what's been going on, though. That he's been regularly bullying you and that your circumstances were ... special. *(Beat)* It was actually the bullying part that scared them off. Doesn't look good to prospective universities these days, apparently, accusations of bullying. *(Beat)* But that's not the point! How could one boy have caused so much damage by himself?! *(Beat)* So, what do you have to say for yourself?

(CONOR shrugs.)

I'm going to need more than that. You seriously hurt him!

CONOR   It wasn't me.

(Beat)

MISS GODFREY   Excuse me?

CONOR   It wasn't me. It was the monster who did it.

MISS GODFREY   The monster.

CONOR   I didn't even touch Harry.

MISS GODFREY   An entire dining hall saw you hitting Harry, Conor. They saw you throwing him over a table! They saw you banging his head against the floor! They heard you yelling about being seen, about not being invisible any more. *(Beat)* I can understand how angry you must be. I mean, we haven't even been able to contact any parent or guardian for you.

CONOR   My dad flew back to America. And Grandma keeps her phone on silent so she won't wake Mum up. Grandma'll probably call you back, though.

MISS GODFREY   School rules dictate immediate exclusion. But how could I do that? How could I do that and still call myself a teacher? With all that you're going through. *(Beat)* We will talk about this, Conor O'Malley. And believe me, we will. But today is not the day – you have bigger things to think about.

CONOR   You're not punishing me?

MISS GODFREY   What purpose could that possibly serve?

(MISS GODFREY exits.)

(CONOR starts walking forward, very slowly.)

(Time passes. We see a series of episodes from CONOR's life over the following four days: DAD on the phone from America; SULLY and ANTON fooling about at school; LILY walking along a corridor; MR MARL and MISS GODFREY in a classroom.)

(The clock turns to 12.07.)

ENSEMBLE   12.07.

(The ENSEMBLE look for the MONSTER, but nothing happens.)

(CONOR continues to walk forward, very slowly.)

(More episodes from CONOR's life: MUM half-asleep at the hospital; GRANDMA drinking water from a disposable cup.)

(Sounds from the nightmare.)

(The clock turns to 12.07.)

ENSEMBLE   12.07.

(The ENSEMBLE wait for the MONSTER, but nothing happens.)

(More sounds from the nightmare.)

(CONOR stops walking.)

CONOR   Where are you?!

26.
A NOTE

(Monday afternoon. School classroom.)

(LILY, SULLY and ANTON enter. The ENSEMBLE become other PUPILS. CONOR sits next to LILY.)

MR MARL   Thank you, Year Eight. And thank you also for your inspirational life writing assignments. What very interesting lives you've led. I was particularly moved by Jessica Sullivan's piece in which she revealed how, at the age of four, she was bitten by a spider—

(SULLY pretends to fire a web from her wrists, like Spiderman.)

       And subsequently developed super powers.

SULLY   Can I show you my spidey senses, sir?

(Beat)

MR MARL   So, storytelling – what have we learned?

LILY   *(Whispering, to CONOR)* Hey!

(CONOR doesn't respond.)

       (Louder) Hey, Conor!

(CONOR turns to LILY. LILY hands him a folded-up note. CONOR unfolds the note and reads it.)

LILY   Line one. I'm sorry for telling everyone about your mum. *(Beat)* Line two. I miss being your friend. *(Beat)* Line three. Are you OK? *(Beat)* Line four, underlined about a hundred times.

(LILY turns and looks at CONOR.)

       I see you.

(CONOR turns and looks at LILY.)

CONOR   Lily—

(MISS GODFREY enters.)

MISS GODFREY Mr Marl, sorry to interrupt. *(Beat)* Conor, could you come with me please?

(CONOR stands up.)

      Bring your bag with you.

(CONOR picks up his bag and goes to MISS GODFREY.)

      Your grandma's here – she's come to pick you up, OK? Come on.

(MISS GODFREY leads CONOR away.)

(MR MARL, LILY, SULLY, ANTON and the PUPILS exit.)

(MISS GODFREY exits.)

27.
100 YEARS

(Monday late afternoon. The hospital.)

(GRANDMA enters.)

CONOR   *(To GRANDMA)* Aren't you coming in?

(MUM enters and sits in a chair. She has more tubes than ever invading her. She is in pain but fighting it.)

GRANDMA   No, I'm not coming in. Give me your bag.

(CONOR hands his rucksack to GRANDMA. GRANDMA exits.)

(CONOR sees MUM. MUM smiles at CONOR.)

MUM   Hi, Con.

CONOR   You're sitting up!

MUM   Come here.

(CONOR half moves towards MUM.)

How you doing, sweetheart?

CONOR   What's going on? Why did Grandma get me out of school?

MUM   I wanted to see you. *(Beat)* And the way the morphine's been sending me off to Cloud Cuckoo Land, I didn't know if I'd get the chance later.

CONOR   You're awake in the evenings sometimes. You could have seen me tonight.

MUM   I wanted to see you now.

(Pause)

CONOR   This is the talk, isn't it? This is…

MUM   Look at me.

(CONOR doesn't respond.)

Look.

(CONOR looks at MUM.)

Conor, I spoke to the doctor this morning – the new treatment isn't working.

CONOR   The one from the yew tree?

MUM   Yes.

CONOR   How can it not be working?

MUM   Things have just moved too fast. It was a faint hope. And now there's this infection—

CONOR   But how can it not be working?

MUM   I know. Looking at that yew tree every day, it felt like I had a friend out there who'd help me if things got to their worst.

CONOR   But it didn't help.

(Pause)

> So what happens now? What's the next treatment?

(Pause)

> There aren't any more treatments.

(Pause)

MUM   I'm sorry, Conor. I've never been more sorry about anything in my life.

CONOR   You said it would work.

MUM   I know.

CONOR   You said. *(Beat)* You believed it would work.

MUM   I know.

CONOR   You lied. You've been lying this whole time.

MUM   I did believe it would work. It's probably what kept me here this long … believing it … so that you would too.

CONOR   You lied.

MUM   I think, deep in your heart, you've always known, haven't you? *(Beat)* It's OK that you're angry, sweetheart. It really, really is. *(Laughs)* I'm pretty angry too, to tell you the truth. But I want you to know – Conor, it's important that you listen to me. Are you listening?

(MUM finds the strength to stand. She goes to CONOR and holds him.)

> You be as angry as you need to be. Don't let anyone tell you otherwise – not your grandma, not your dad, no one. And if you need to break things, then by God, you break them – you break them good and hard.

(CONOR still can't look at MUM.)

82

And if, one day … you look back and you feel bad for being so angry, if you feel bad for being so angry at me that you couldn't even speak to me, then you have to know, Conor, you have to know that it was OK. It was OK. That I knew. I know, OK? I know everything you need to tell me without you having to say it out loud. All right?

(CONOR nods, still unable to look at her.)

(MUM feels a sudden pain in her side and drops to the floor.)

I'm sorry, Conor. *(Beat)* I'm going to need some more painkillers.

(MUM returns to her chair and administers some intravenous drugs.)

I wish I had a hundred years – a hundred years I could give to you.

(MUM falls asleep. CONOR looks at her sleeping.)

(GRANDMA enters.)

GRANDMA   Conor…? Conor?

CONOR   I want to go home.

GRANDMA   What?!

CONOR   My home – the one with the yew tree.

GRANDMA   Why?! What on earth could—?

CONOR   There's something I need to do.

GRANDMA   All right. But I can't leave your mother for long. I'll take you home and pick you up in an hour. One hour, all right?

(GRANDMA exits.)

28.
WHAT'S THE USE OF YOU?

(Monday night. Outside, at the back of CONOR's house.)

(CONOR goes to the yew tree.)

CONOR   Wake up!

(The tree does not respond.)

(CONOR hits the yew tree.)

            Wake up!

(The tree still doesn't respond.)

(CONOR kicks the yew tree.)

            I said, wake up! I don't care what time it is!

(The MONSTER enters, up high in the tree.)

            It didn't work! You said the yew tree would heal her and it didn't!

MONSTER   I said if she could be healed, the yew tree would do it. It seems she could not.

(CONOR attacks the yew tree.)

CONOR   Heal her! You have to heal her!

MONSTER   Conor...

CONOR   What's the use of you if you can't heal her?

(CONOR continues to attack the tree.)

            Just stupid stories and getting me into trouble and everyone looking at me like I've got a disease—

MONSTER   You are the one who called me, Conor O'Malley. You are the one with the answers to these questions.

(The MONSTER hoists CONOR into the air.)

CONOR   *(Crying)* If I called you … it was to save her! It was
             to heal her!

MONSTER   I did not come to heal her. I came to heal you.

CONOR   Me? *(Beat)* I don't need healing. My mum's the one
             who—

(CONOR collapses on the floor.)

             (Quietly) Help me.

MONSTER   It is time for the fourth tale.

CONOR   No! That's not what I meant! There are more
             important things happening!

MONSTER   Yes. Yes, there are.

(The MONSTER picks up CONOR and carries him into the nightmare.)

29.
THE FOURTH TALE

(The ENSEMBLE transform the space.)

(A cliff edge appears.)

(The MONSTER forces CONOR to stay in the nightmare.)

CONOR   No! No! Please!

MONSTER   It is time for the fourth tale.

CONOR   I don't know any tales!

(CONOR struggles to escape.)

             Go away! Go away!

MONSTER   If you do not tell it, then I shall have to tell it for
             you. And believe me, you do not want that! *(Beat)*
             Tell it!

(CONOR is overpowered by the force of the nightmare.)

CONOR   This is just my nightmare!

MONSTER   This is your truth!

CONOR   Get me out of here! Please! I have to get back to my mum.

(Beat)

MONSTER   But she is already here.

(MUM enters, high on the cliff edge, unperturbed.)

MUM   Conor! Look at this! Isn't it beautiful!

CONOR   Mum! You have to get out of here! You have to run!

MUM   I'm fine, sweetheart – there's nothing to worry about.

CONOR   Mum, run! Please, run!

MUM   I'm fine, Conor!

CONOR   No!

(CONOR goes towards MUM on the cliff edge.)

MUM   *(Still unperturbed)* You have to see this! It's so beautiful here! There's nothing to be afraid of! Conor…!

(MUM inches towards the edge of the cliff, suddenly realizing she might be in peril.)

             Wait! Conor! *(Beat)* What is this place?!

(CONOR joins MUM on the cliff edge.)

CONOR   Mum!

(MUM suddenly falls from the cliff edge.)

MUM   No!

(CONOR throws himself towards MUM and catches hold of her hands. MUM dangles feet first from the cliff edge.)

Help me! Don't let go!

CONOR   I won't! I promise! I'll never let go!

(MUM begins to slip from CONOR's grasp.)

MUM   Please, Conor! Hold on to me!

CONOR   I will! *(To MONSTER)* Help me! I can't hold onto her!

(The MONSTER does nothing, just watches.)

MUM   Conor!

(MUM's hands slip further from CONOR's.)

               Conor!

CONOR   Mum!

MUM   I'm slipping!

(MUM screams.)

CONOR   Please! Please!

MONSTER   And here is the fourth tale.

CONOR   Shut up! *Help* me!

MONSTER   Here is the truth of Conor O'Malley.

(MUM screams again, slipping further from CONOR's grasp.)

               It is now or never. You must speak the truth.

CONOR   No!

MONSTER   You *must*.

CONOR   No!

(MUM slips from CONOR's grasp and falls into the abyss.)

               No!

(Pause)

MONSTER   The tale is not yet told.

CONOR   Take me out of here. I need to see my mum.

MONSTER   She is no longer here, Conor. You let her go.

CONOR   This is just a nightmare. This isn't the truth.

MONSTER   It *is* the truth. And you know it is. You let her go.

CONOR   She fell. I couldn't hold on to her any more. She got so heavy.

MONSTER   And so you let her go.

CONOR   I didn't let her go! She fell!

MONSTER   You must tell the truth or you will never leave this nightmare. You will be trapped here alone for the rest of your life.

CONOR   Please let me go! *(Beat)* Help me!

MONSTER   Speak the truth or stay here forever.

CONOR   I don't know what you mean.

MONSTER   You do know.

(Beat)

CONOR   I can't.

MONSTER   You can.

CONOR   Please don't make me say it.

MONSTER   You let her go.

(CONOR closes his eyes tightly, then nods.)

    You could have held on for longer, but you let her fall. You loosened your grip and let the nightmare take her.

(CONOR nods again.)

    You wanted her to fall.

CONOR   No!

MONSTER   You wanted her to go.

CONOR   No!

MONSTER   You must speak the truth, and you must speak it
             now, Conor O'Malley! Say it! You must!

CONOR   It'll kill me if I do.

MONSTER   It will kill you if you do not. You must say it.

CONOR   I can't.

MONSTER   You let her go. Why?

*(CONOR feels himself suffocating, as though the nightmare is trying to
kill him.)*

             Why, Conor? Tell me why, before it's too late!

(CONOR feels the truth begin to eat him and burn him.)

CONOR   I can't stand it any more! I can't stand knowing that
             she'll go! I just want it to be over! I want it to be
             finished!

*(CONOR collapses. The truth eats the world around him, wiping
everything away.)*

30.
LIFE AFTER DEATH

(A little later. Outside, near CONOR's house.)

(The MONSTER goes to CONOR and holds him in his arms.)

(CONOR opens his eyes.)

CONOR   Why didn't it kill me? I deserve the worst.

MONSTER   Do you?

CONOR   I've known forever she wasn't going to make it,
             almost from the beginning. She said she was getting
             better because that's what I wanted to hear. And I
             believed her. Except I didn't.

MONSTER   No.

CONOR   And I started to think how much I wanted it
                    to be over. How much I just wanted to stop
                    having to think about it. How I couldn't stand
                    the waiting any more. I couldn't stand how alone
                    it made me feel.

(CONOR cries.)

MONSTER   And a part of you wished it would just end, even if it
                    meant losing her.

(CONOR nods.)

                    And the nightmare began. The nightmare that
                    always ended with—

CONOR   I let her go. I could have held on, but I let her go.

MONSTER   And that is the truth.

CONOR   I didn't mean it, though! I didn't mean to let her go!
                    And now it's for real! Now she's going to die and it's
                    all my fault!

MONSTER   And that is not the truth at all.

CONOR   It's my fault. I let her go. It's my fault.

MONSTER   It is not your fault.

CONOR   It is.

MONSTER   You were simply wishing for the end of pain – your
                    own pain. An end to how it isolated you. It is the
                    most human wish of all.

CONOR   I didn't mean it.

MONSTER   You did. But you also did not.

CONOR   How can both be true?

MONSTER   Because humans are complicated beasts. *(Beat)*
                    How can a queen be both a good witch and a bad
                    witch? How can a prince be a murderer and a
                    saviour? How can an apothecary be evil-tempered

90

but right-thinking, and a parson be wrong-thinking but good-hearted? And how can invisible men make themselves more lonely by being seen?

CONOR I don't know. Your stories never made any sense to me.

MONSTER The answer is that it does not matter what you think. Because your mind will contradict itself a hundred times each day. You wanted her to go at the same time you were desperate for me to save her. Your mind will believe comforting lies while also knowing the painful truths that make those lies necessary. And your mind will punish you for believing both.

CONOR But how do you fight it? How do you fight all the different stuff inside?

MONSTER By speaking the truth. As you spoke it just now.

CONOR That's it?

MONSTER You think it is easy? You were willing to die rather than speak it.

CONOR Because what I thought was so wrong.

MONSTER It was not wrong. It was only a thought. It was not an action.

(Beat)

CONOR I'm so tired. I'm so tired of all this.

MONSTER Then sleep. There is time.

CONOR Is there? I need to see my mum.

MONSTER You will. I promise.

(The MONSTER lays CONOR down to sleep.)

CONOR Will you be there?

MONSTER I will. It will be the final steps of my walking.

(Pause)

CONOR   Why do you always come at 12.07?

(CONOR falls asleep.)

31.
SOMETHING IN COMMON

(Monday night, just after 11 p.m. Outside, at the yew tree, near CONOR's house.)

(CONOR is sleeping at the foot of the yew tree.)

(GRANDMA enters searching for CONOR.)

GRANDMA   Conor…?! Conor?!

(GRANDMA continues to search for CONOR.)

                Conor?!

(GRANDMA discovers CONOR. GRANDMA goes to CONOR and hugs him hard. CONOR wakes up.)

                Oh, thank God! Thank God! Conor! Conor…

(CONOR sits up, still coming round.)

                Where have you been?! I've been searching for hours! I've been frantic, Conor! What the hell were you thinking?!

CONOR   There was something I needed to do.

GRANDMA   No time. We have to go! We have to go now!

(GRANDMA hurries CONOR away.)

(The sound of a car setting off in a hurry.)

(CONOR and GRANDMA are in the car, journeying to the hospital.)

                Conor, you can't just…

CONOR   Grandma—

GRANDMA   Don't. Just don't.

(Pause)

(A car horn sounds.)

CONOR   Grandma?!

(Pause)

Grandma, I'm so sorry.

(Beat)

GRANDMA   It doesn't matter. It doesn't matter.

CONOR   It doesn't?

GRANDMA   Of *course* it doesn't. You know, Conor? You and me? Not the most natural fit, are we?

CONOR   No. I guess not.

GRANDMA   I guess not either. But we're going to have to learn, you know.

CONOR   I know.

GRANDMA   Yes, you do know, don't you? Of course you do. But you know what? We have something in common.

CONOR   We do?

GRANDMA   Oh, yes.

CONOR   What's that?

(The car comes to a stop – GRANDMA and CONOR have arrived at the hospital.)

GRANDMA   Your mum. That's what we have in common.

(CONOR and GRANDMA look at each other.)

We have to hurry.

(CONOR and GRANDMA get out of the car and rush into the hospital.)

32.
THE TRUTH

(A hospital room. Just before midnight.)

(NB This is the first time we see anything approaching a naturalistic set – a real hospital bed, monitors, drips etc.)

(A digital clock shows 12.02 a.m.)

(MUM enters, lying in a hospital bed, completely exhausted, approaching death.)

(A NURSE enters.)

(GRANDMA rushes in, followed by CONOR.)

NURSE   *(To GRANDMA)* It's all right. There's still time.

(The NURSE exits.)

(GRANDMA takes MUM's hand in hers. She kisses the hand and rocks back and forth.)

MUM   Mum…?

GRANDMA   I'm here, darling. Conor's here too.

MUM   Is he?

(Pause)

CONOR   I'm here, Mum.

(CONOR stands away from the bed. MUM reaches out her hand for CONOR.)

(The MONSTER appears.)

MONSTER   Here is the end of the tale.

CONOR   What do I do?

(The MONSTER places its hands on CONOR's shoulders.)

MONSTER   All you have to do is tell the truth.

CONOR   I'm afraid to.

MONSTER   Of course you are afraid. And yet you will still do it.

CONOR   How does the story end?

MONSTER   If you speak the truth you will be able to face
               whatever comes.

CONOR   *(To the MONSTER)* You'll stay? You'll stay until...

MONSTER   I will stay.

(The MONSTER gently urges CONOR towards MUM.)

*(CONOR goes to MUM and takes her hand. MUM opens her eyes briefly
and looks at CONOR, then closes her eyes again.)*

CONOR   *(To MUM)* I don't want you to go.

MUM   I know, my love. I know.

CONOR   I don't want you to go.

*(CONOR climbs on to the bed and puts his arms around MUM, holding on
to her tightly. GRANDMA continues to hold MUM's hand.)*

MONSTER   And so the story ends with the boy holding tightly
               on to his mother. And by doing so, he could finally
               let her go.

(CONOR continues to hold tightly on to MUM.)

(The clock ticks over to show 12.07 a.m.)

(Blackout.)

END OF ACT TWO

THE END

DISCOVER MORE FROM PATRICK NESS

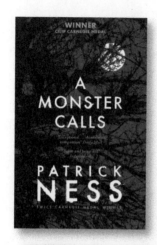

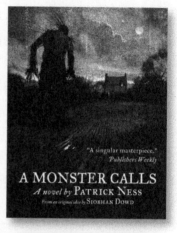

"Patrick Ness is an insanely beautiful writer."
JOHN GREEN